THIS ISSUE

INTRODUCTION TO PATHOS

What you hold in your hand is the humble effort of a few like-minded people who want to change the world for the better. Unlike others with a similar aspiration, we are not attempting to eradicate world hunger, argue for economic equality, or promote similar issues concerning social justice and human welfare. While these are all admirable pursuits, what it is we seek to do is change the way people think. We want to change the way people see the world, and what it is they believe about God, themselves, and the universe.

Perhaps the most important thing about a person is what he believes. It literally makes him who he is. It guides his life and informs all his thoughts and decisions. For good or ill what a man believes is the substance of his being. That being so, to change the world in a deep and meaningful way, you must first change how and what people believe.

Popular belief today suggests that faith and culture, especially as it applies to public life, should be separate. But if people are made by what they believe, and those same people are what make up a culture, then faith is an inextricable part of that culture. It is where that intersection takes place, where faith and culture come together, influence one another in positive and negative ways, that is the subject and focus of this magazine.

So we present to you what we hope is but the first of many offerings. Inside you will find articles, fiction, poetry, essays, and some un-classifiables. Knowing that to change how people think and believe you must appeal to the heart as well as the mind, we include these products of the imagination. For what touches the heart so well as poetry, story and art?

This being an art in itself, we expect an increased excellence of the craft and the finished product with the passage of practice and time. So as you look over this and judge its contents, think both on what it is, and what it could be. If it challenges you in any of your beliefs, enlightens, or enriches you in any way, then our efforts are a success. And if you are transformed for the better, then we have aided the work of the Master of all good art, and in aiding him, we have served the good of all.

And if in the process you develop a little pathos—passion, depth of feeling, a fire for life—then that is good too.

Enjoy,

Robert W Cely

DELUSIONAL OR KANGAROOSIONAL?

BY GRAHAM KELL

We all have an everyday world draped in the mundane curtains of laundry and lunchtimes. It's where we spend most waking hours. Maybe that's why we pull back the curtain in our sleeping hours and let our minds roam another world, of nonsensical creatures and fantastical beaches...until we wake up, that is. Then the realism of the first world out-yells the idealism of the second. Myth is that magical thread that connects the two; the seen to the unseen. That's why we need it in stories, hear it in ballads, and watch it in movies—because we long for it in life.

But it's a thin thread easily broken by adult worries, leaving us stranded on this side of the curtain.

This is why I love Dr. Seuss. He was a master of myth for children, whose thread is still rope-thick and everyday world still dreamlike.

It's hard to pick a favourite Seuss tale, but *Horton Hears a Who* comes close. It's about an elephant who hears a creature too small to see. Other animals think he's delusional. In the movie version, a kangaroo tells Horton, "If you can't see, hear, or feel something, it doesn't exist. And believing is not something we tolerant here. Our community has standards Horton. If you want to remain a part of it, I recommend you follow them!"

I sometimes cop the same scalding for my belief in God. "If you can't see it, it doesn't exist, so if you want to be a part of this world Graham, you better follow our standards!" But, to quote Horton, "What if there is someone out there, looking down on our world?" What if there is Someone we can't see?

I worked with kangaroos for many years and have to say, they're not unlike the kangaroo in *Horton*. As a ranger, I managed their lives and monitored their health. They always assumed they were in charge. Not once did they realize that a Ranger who lived down a road they'd not traveled, knew and cared for their needs.

Out of sight, out of mind. "If you can't see, hear, or feel something, it doesn't exist."

We kangaroos rarely realize there's a Ranger who lives up a road we've not traveled. We assume we're in charge, yet He oversees our lives. We may disagree with His decisions, but our denial of His presence makes as much difference to Him as my kangaroos' denial of my existence made to me!

This is why I love the Scriptures. They pull back the curtain in a very Seussian way. They give a glimpse up a road we haven't yet hopped. They weave words that form a thread connecting two worlds; this natural kangaroo paddock with the supernatural place behind the curtain.

In the world of myth, C. S. Lewis is for adults what Dr. Seuss is for children. Echoing Horton, Lewis once wrote, "There may be Natures piled upon Natures, each supernatural to the one beneath it." An interesting thought and a blurry line. May we not cross it and become delusional, but may we not ignore it and become kangaroosional!

Of Science
and
Scientism

By Jim Yarbrough

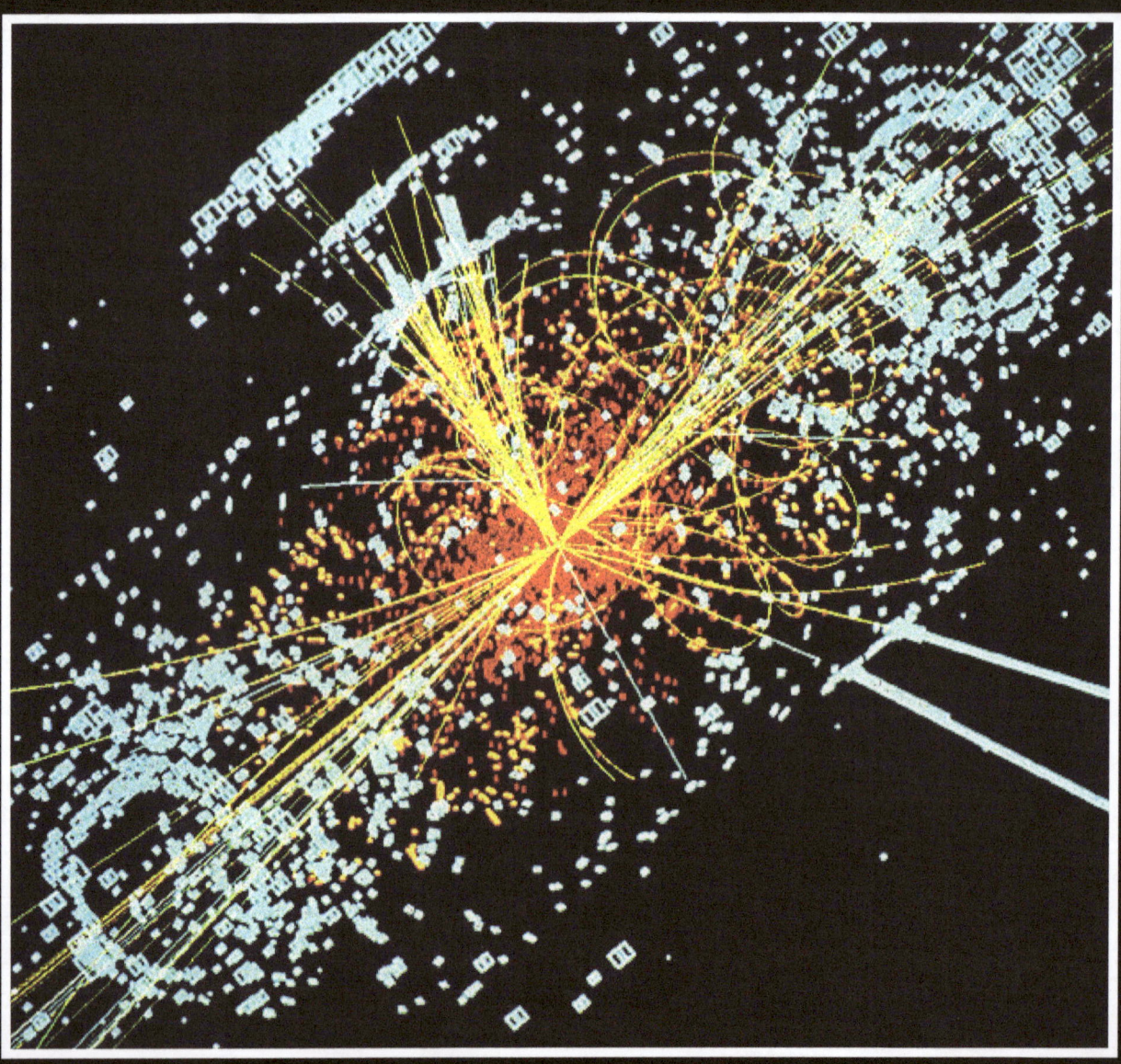

In our silly times, outlandish messages can quickly become impediments to clear thinking.

For example, take the following:

M-theory renders philosophy meaningless.
The science is settled.
Christianity is at war with science.

The first, an opinion attributed to a world-renowned cosmologist. The second, a quote from a senior U.S. Government official about climate change. The third, a pillar of worldly anomie.

What can a little thinking do to help sort through these?

First, what do the above statements have in common? Answer: They all directly endorse or reflect the big idea of scientism.

Scientism is the belief that science alone is sufficient to reveal all relevant truth to people. Like Christianity, scientism is a worldview. Scientism aims to drive all thoughts and pursuits, even those beyond the strictly scientific (as in statement 1). It is an outgrowth of positivism and logical positivism beginning in the 19th century, from which any pursuit not clearly steeped in empiricism or logic is judged invalid.

But importantly, science is not scientism. Science is a practice that utilizes a rigorous methodology, i.e. the scientific method. It is therefore not a worldview and not comparable to Christianity or scientism. And, incidentally, because science is a practice that constantly questions the universe around us in a continuous, knowledge-enhancing process, it is never really "settled" – even when scientism might want it to be. So, ironically, in attempting to bolster some existing, preferred knowledge as closure, statement two negated the nature of science itself. Additionally, it also overlooked the significant, new findings about climate change and "short-term climate forcers," which were contemporaneously emerging with this unfortunate statement. It is no secret that scientism's undercutting of science troubles many in the scientific community.

Third, while it may be convenient for scientism to paint Christianity, one of its prime worldview rivals, as irrelevant and antagonistic to science (see statement 3), it is fundamentally inaccurate to claim such. A recent survey found millions of evangelical Christians are scientists in the U.S., and a greater percentage of those individuals than in the overall population believe religion and science are compatible. Galileo, Kepler, Copernicus, Boyle, Leibniz, and many other Enlightenment scientists were dedicated Christians, and others such as Newton and Pascal saw Christian belief as a major underpinning of scientific inquiry. In fact, many major Renaissance scientists were

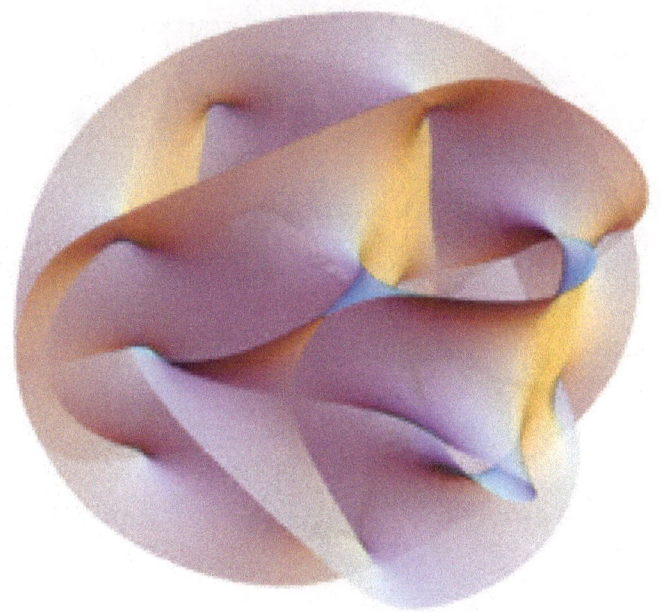

Christians confident their loving God created a largely predictable universe, one where their experimentation and theory-building could proceed logically and be rewarded. Christian belief is certainly not at war with science.

Take-aways from this short exercise? Science is an exciting endeavor and has benefitted humankind immensely, but science is definitely not scientism; by contrast, if science is marked by rigorous and healthy knowledge acquisition, then scientism is characterized by unjustified extrapolating that leaves little room for questions or challenges to its narrow view; and Christians have been – and continue to be – enthusiastic science practitioners and researchers.

THE GRAND
MYTH

By Robert W Cely

Men are shaped by the stories and songs around them.

~ Neil Gaiman

A few years ago, to celebrate the 200th birthday of Charles Darwin, a group of billboards went up around town funded by the atheist organization, Freedom From Religion. The group is well known for their efforts to remove any public expressions of religious devotion, which made these particular billboards noteworthy. It wasn't the fact that they celebrated Darwin's birthday that made them interesting, but the language they chose to use.

"Praise Darwin," the signs urged, written in a scroll-type font and complete with a picture of the patron saint. And while I am certain that the people at Freedom From Religion thought themselves quit clever, and a bit ironic with the display, it belied a real sense of devotion that they feel towards the landmark figure.

As much as they might deny it, your real ardent atheists regard figures like Darwin, Copernicus and Nietzsche - all perceived challengers to the religious establishment - with a kind of reverence that can best be described as veneration. Even if there is no direct worship of Darwin, the attitude presented toward him is worshipful, his words considered canon and his life an exemplary model. It makes it seem that even forceful unbelievers can't help but act religious sometimes.

To any who honestly study human nature, this should come as no surprise. Human beings, we are beginning to understand, are naturally religious creatures. Or maybe this is something we are re-learning. Earlier ages never would have denied people's natural religious inclinations.

Today though, there is a movement to remove all traces of religion from any person or institution even vaguely affiliated with government or has any public persona at all. These groups, like Freedom From Religion, want to create a world virtually devoid of faith. Religion is being forcefully shoved into the most private moments of the individu-al, unable to inform any though or action taken outside a house or church. They tolerate religion only as long as it has no effective impact on the world at large. If the momentum of removing faith from public life continues unabated, then devotion will soon be reduced to the realm of privately held thoughts. Already there is great protest if religious conviction influences any public decision.

The attempt to remove religion from public life presents us with two difficult problems. The first is that the individuals who make up the government still retain their freedom of religion, even as functionaries of the State. Secondly, and more problematic, is the fact that humans are naturally religious. All thought and activity is guided by some set of values that can be considered religious in nature. If it is not one, then it will be another. Humans cannot help but act on religious principle. Even as some try to be guided by values that are secular, and purely based on reason and science, they only accomplish setting a new set of values that is as inherently religious as the one rejected.

In other words, all men are religious, and cannot help being so.

Of course, this idea hinges on your definition of religion. That question is one that can, and has, filled up book after book with answers as various as the authors presenting. But there seems to be some agreement that religion is, at the very least, a worldview or outlook. How we choose to interpret events, what we think about the world, what we believe the nature of reality is, the purpose of life, the right way to live; these are things that make up a religion. And like opinions, everyone has one.

Specifically, the ideas that make up a religion are extremely basic in nature, the answers forming the foundation of a particular worldview. How was the universe created? How was man created? What is the nature and composition of reality? And of course, is there a God? From there we answer less basic, but questions of more immediate urgency. What is the purpose of man? What is good? How will creation end? Is there life after death?

The interesting and telling thing to note about fundamental questions is their nebulous, and largely unprovable, character. There is no way to reach certainty about these matters. The answers to these questions cannot be proven like other facts. They are either inaccessible to the senses and scientific study, or they deal with historical events so distant that we can never know for sure what really happened.

Just consider any fundamental question. Is there a God? As much as we would like certainty, there is simply no way to achieve it. For if there is a God, then He willfully chooses to keep himself hidden for the most part. He doesn't appear over mountaintops at an appointed schedule, nor does he rearrange the stars to write us messages in the night sky. Even of those who claim to speak to God, it isn't a conversation anyone else is privy to. Only the prophet hears God. The mass miracles we hear about in the Bible are rare. For believers, any certainty about God's existence is elusive.

The unbeliever has even greater difficulty. Although the lack of divine appearances at first works for the atheist's argument, some unanswered questions quickly threaten. The origin of the universe, the origin of life, the emergence of consciousness, morality, the historical validity of certain religious claims, and the ability for men to act altruistically all have proved difficult for the unbeliever to answer and have required increasingly elaborate and unbelievable theoretical schemes.

A perfect example of this is the question of the origin of life. The godless universe posits life not being created, but emerging from the basic chemicals of a young earth. The problem is that these chemicals are inorganic, and as of now it is difficult to conceive of how organic, living things emerged and evolved from the inorganic. The speculation has been vast and complex to answer this difficult question. Some have even proposed such outlandish and ridiculous scenarios like chemicals attached to growing crystals in order to form the basic compounds of life.

While proving the existence of God may be impossible, disproving His existence is equally beyond the reach of the human mind. Fundamental questions are usually questions that have no clear answers.

At the same time the answers to the fundamentals form the basis for any outlook on the world and life. These questions must have some sort of answer before any other question can be entertained. We all have them, though mostly we give them no consideration. They are the assumptions we have rattling around in our heads unaware, yet they inform and guide us without our knowledge of their influence. They are much like the brain functions that control our unconscious activity. We may not be aware of our brains regulating breath and heartbeat, but they are there and absolutely essential.

In the same way our fundamental beliefs inform all of our other attitudes and beliefs. How we treat others, what we consider acceptable and good, what is worth fighting for, what is just and fair, what is valuable, what and how we eat, how we interact with others, what we study, how we spend our leisure time; all of these and more are directed by the fundamental beliefs we carry in us about the nature of man and the world.

Try as we might, we cannot gain any certainty about the fundamental questions of life. This is why we distinguish our deeply held convictions as beliefs. No one says, "I believe the grass is green," "I believe in gravity," or "I believe force equals mass times acceleration."

The situation certainly makes things difficult for us. We all have fundamental beliefs that shape our world view, and are the most basic and important of our beliefs. But these fundamentals are beyond proof and certainty. The things that are available to sense and reason, what we see, feel and hear, are reasonably certain, but tell us nothing about the foundational nature of reality.

Some would certainly argue that evolution and the big bang are beyond speculation and firmly entrenched in the realm of fact, and therefore can form a certain basis for foundational beliefs. Any who would claim this either willfully or ignorantly overlooks the extremely speculative nature of both. They both study unobservable, unique phenomenon, about which we can never achieve certainty. Even if the event could be recreated in a laboratory, it still wouldn't prove that was what actually happened. What could happen and what did happen are rarely the same.

Whatever happened at the beginning of the universe and when man first emerged those many years ago left some traces of itself behind. But what these traces mean is open to interpretation. And how we interpret the evidence depends wholly on our fundamental beliefs, already in place when we examine the evidence supposedly giving us a glimpse into the fundamental nature of the universe.

In other words, we cannot look at any evidence to shape our fundamental beliefs about the world, since it is our beliefs that shape how we interpret that evidence. A believer and atheist will look at the same body of evidence and come to vastly different conclusions. One will say the laws of the universe prove there is no god. The other that a lawful universe is indisputable proof that God exists.

It should become quickly evident how impossible it is to prove any an-

ment of heavy rhetoric, mockery and suppression by both parties. The most avid evolutionists may be the worst offenders. Besides being the party of the ruling idea, they hypocritically violate the principles of open, scientific inquiry. Every week we hear of these supposedly open-minded academics use strong-arm tactics to suppress any study or evidence that might threaten their sacred theory of human origins. The behavior displayed is typical of one insisting on the rightness of an indefensible position.

The truth is that the nature of unique events make them unprovable, especially unique events beyond the reach of eye witness. All we can know for sure from the fossil record is that there once existed strange creatures with skeletons similar to our own. Beyond this is speculation. That human beings evolved from these is far from certain, no matter how forcefully it may be insisted.

The mythology of a purely material, rational world is a mass fiction perpetuated by the adherents of materialism.

swer to fundamental questions. Not only are they beyond the access of sensory investigation, but the very means by which we interpret data is dictated by the worldview we possess, already in place when we encounter that data. So of course, we will interpret that data in a way that conforms to what we already believe. It is a self-sustaining cycle, unable to be broken by access to argument and reason alone, and beyond the reach of experimental science.

In the argument over human origins, both sides are aware of the unprovable nature of their positions, creationists as well as evolutionists. This is why you see the employ-

There is something other than reason, evidence and argument that influence and shape a person's basic, foundational beliefs, that shape his religion. It is beyond the reach of the rational, housed deep within the pre-rational spaces of mind where we form these perceptions. Much has to do with culture of origin, and more people than I would like to admit simply believes what everyone else around them believes, for good or ill.

But almost everyone can be swayed. Ultimately, it is not any rationality or soundness of argument that will convince. Deeper in our psyche dwells the impulse to believe, much deeper than the conscious mind that weighs the merits of argument. If we could peer into the soul, into the seat of faith, we would find ideas not expressed in reason, but in poetry. The soul sees the world more as a novel than a textbook. In other words, our most basic beliefs are not theology, but mythology.

When people choose between religious ideas, if they choose at all, it is conflicting mythologies they choose between. Which story of humanity and the cosmos rings most true, rings best to them? Which story is their story? Which narrative of the universe reflects the temperament of their own soul?

For some it will be an angry and exacting God. For others they accept a kind God. Some resonate with an all-knowing God while others prefer the aloof and distant God. The decision is made on a pre-rational basis. If we do not

universe that tout themselves to be above opinion and dispute, are as irrational as any other. The very idea of a universe that can be ultimately known by science and reason is a key component in secular mythology. Because some things can be known by reason and science doesn't mean they all can. To believe that one day science will unlock all mysteries is an article of faith. Like the Baptist who awaits Rapture, the secularist who hopes in the eventual triumph of science, espouses a religious, not rational, hope. For there is nothing more irrational and religious as hope.

Because secularism lacks the colorful stories you find in traditional cultures, that does not make their foundational beliefs any less myth. You will find stories there if you look, but they dress in the sophisticated clothes of scientific certainty. The Norse myth tells of a universe growing

In a word, mythology is a search; it is something that combines a recurrent desire with a recurrent doubt, mixing a most hungry sincerity in the idea of seeking for a place with a most dark and deep and mysterious levity about all the places found.

~ G.K. Chesterton
The Everlasting Man

follow the myth of our surrounding culture then we follow the one that matches how we view ourselves, or we think the world should be.

Positive people tend to adopt a positive mythology while negative people adopt a negative mythology.

That is not to say that because we make pre-rational decisions about what we believe that all beliefs are equally false, or have an equally random chance of being true. All ideas are not equal and all myth is not equally true. What it does mean is that we must take a different, humbler approach to our apprehension of truth. The universe is fundamentally mysterious and largely unknowable. Much about foundational reality can be known, just not in the way we are taught and encouraged to approach it.

This also means that the so-called rational views of the

out of the great tree, Yggdrasill. Christianity hints at a multi-layered reality, culminating in the highest heaven. The myths of secularism insists on a purely material world, ruled by unbending laws that run the universe and the individual man like a machine. Far from being original, this outlook, this mechanism, is strictly Calvinistic in nature. All things are determined by the laws of the universe and the irresistible will of cause and effect operating on a molecular level. Human freedom is negligent. Man is ruled by his nature and by what went before him as absolutely as a machine is run by its design.

The mythology of a purely material, rational world is a mass fiction perpetuated by the adherents of materialism. Far from being the open-minded, free-thinking, liberated outlook that its mythology promotes, it is a narrow-minded and exclusive worldview, tolerating no dissent. It forc-

crime and disease. The story soars with religious fervor, promising a paradise that all faiths promise. Except in this one, there is no force higher than man, so he is a god unto himself, and able to indulge all his whims freely. Woe to any who would interfere.

This is the myth that shapes and informs our world today. Almost every problem that we encounter in our increasingly immoral, self-centered, deluded and sick society can be traced back to the stories of secular mythology. The myth that makes man supreme can have little option but to allow him free reign to his desires and confirmation of the infantile fantasy of being the center of the universe. It should come as no surprise then, that each generation is raised more selfish and self-indulgent than the last.

We have no choice but to believe - believe something. The universe, as it is, offers no assurance. But life demands we have faith.

That this is true anyone can discover for himself. Examine any system that claims to have fundamental truths, and very soon you will reach questions that have no answer; a place where the most ardent believers try to hurry you past, wave away any objections, even blush with embarrassment, or more likely grow forceful and insistent that only an idiot would believe otherwise or the alternative is far worse.

They do this to cover the mystery at the heart of the universe. They cover it like we cover our nakedness. Even though our naked bodies are our true bodies, and the clothes merely the veneer we present to the world, we would never walk unclothed out in daylight.

In the same way, the naked mystery of the universe is the true nature of things. We cover it with the clothing of arrogant certainty and convoluted arguments that always crumble with time and wear. So we change the clothing of our ideas frequently, lest the thrill and terror of the cosmos be laid bare before us.

Our own essential nature is just as mysterious as that of the universe. Perhaps that is why we often seem strangers to ourselves. But that mystery is essential to our ultimate identity. And therein we find that it is not our thoughts that make us who we are, but our faith.

es thoughts into a narrow funnel so that conclusions are almost inevitable and variety nearly impossible. Maybe this is the appeal of materialistic-mechanism. Its absolute nature leaves no room for dissent and pretends no doubt. It boasts unshakable certainty, and though it may give man a grim place in the universe, that place is beyond question. Or that is what they would have us think.

The most ardent atheist and empiricist founds his world on myth, as unprovable as any other. It is a narrative of a cold and uncaring universe and a lucky mammal that beats the odds with the power of his larger brain, rising to become master of his world. The story even projects into the future, prophesying when this clever mammal will use his brain - the true seat of humanity in this mythos - to overcome all the obstacles of this uncaring universe. One day, death itself will be outsmarted alongside hunger,

Worlds Collide

fiction by Anthony Horvath

I was scared as hell of my father, and, in my mind, for good reason.

First of all, it is a known fact that he hates me. Second of all, my most vivid memory remains being struck upside the head at the dinner table so hard that I nearly fell out of my chair. If I had been an onlooker, I know I would have laughed. I was eating mashed potatoes and corn and these spewed out of my mouth and splattered on the wall behind me. It had to have been a funny sight. My father's face, however, was humorless.

"Don't ever say something like that to your mother, or any woman for that matter, ever again. You hear?" he snarled, gesturing at me with the fork in his hand, aimed, as it seemed to me, right for my eyeballs. Between bites, I had repeated a comment that I had heard from one of the other boys while walking home from school. All of my friends laughed. I didn't really understand the joke; something about somebody's mother and meat, so as I reached for the roast beef, it seemed like a good thing to say.

You've gotta understand that this was the first and only thing he had said to me in a month, and it was accompa-nied by a blow to my head. Some would welcome being ignored by their father, and perhaps I also would revel in his indifference, if not for the fact that this clear sign of his hatred is punctuated by a physical rebuke.

I didn't see my father much. He was already gone in the morning when I woke up. He was often home in time for dinner, but he never talked while he ate. When din-ner was over, he disappeared into his bedroom to watch the television. Those thirty minutes of supper time and a few hours on the weekend pretty much accounted for all of our time together. My mother was much more in-volved, but after dinner she also would disappear for a bit to watch television, afterwards appearing to put me and my sister to bed. I knew from early on that she loved him, through and through. I was afraid of him, but there was no hint that she was. I honestly couldn't understand it.

I have this teacher that also hates my guts. Mr. Cavana-ugh taught social studies and had this ridiculous idea that people should be interested in what he was teaching. I made a mistake in the first weeks of school, answering one of his questions when no one else even raised their hand. Mr. Cavanaugh had been impressed and ever since he would come at me for answers, and my friends would giggle, so I started feeding him the wrong answers. Instead of leaving me alone, he got angry, and came at me even more. It's not my fault I was the only kid in class that read the textbook in just a couple of days. This was supposed to spare me loads of work later on when all the other kids were struggling to keep up with the weekly readings, but it had never happened before that the fact that I already knew what we were going to learn was used against me.

Mr. Cavanaugh was a tall, string of a man. He had a mustache that threatened to curl up on the ends but otherwise kept his face clean-shaved. His hair was cut short, so short that the arms of his glasses could be completely seen as they arched behind his ears. Some called him Green-Bean Cavanaugh, and it was easy to see why. There was no question in my mind that even a gentle breeze could topple him over, and there were some jokes about creating a wind machine in class just to see how much he could take.

There was no question that he was smart. The rumor was that he was so smart that he had been driven out of wherever he taught last and our school was the only one who would take him. When he stood up to deliver the lecture, I knew it was from the book, because I had read the book, but his book was closed up behind him. He did it all from memory. He was always jazzing it up with personal stories but he could never hide the fact that he was still just a teacher. Teachers lived boring, inconsequential lives, and no lying about it to try to make class interesting was going to fool us.

The day after my dad smashed mashed potatoes out of my mouth things took a turn for the worse in Mr. Cavanaugh's class.

"You got a 'C' on this test," Mr. Cavanaugh said to me, loud enough for everyone to hear.

"Yea, so what," I growled back.

"You're an 'A' student, Caleb. You have to work harder to get a 'C' than others have to work to get an 'A.' This is unacceptable," Mr. Cavanaugh said.

The notion that my classmates would regard me as competent was unacceptable. Damage control was in order.

"I ain't no 'A' student. Your tests are too hard. Make them easier and then I'll get an 'A,'" I retorted.

"My tests are only hard for those who don't do the work. But you've done the work, haven't you, Caleb?" Mr. Cavanaugh jabbed.

I shrugged. "I don't know what you're talking about."

"I'll tell you what I'm talking about. You're coming back after school today and correcting your answers to these questions," he said.

"No, I'm going home after school, same as always."

"Then you'll get a detention."

"Do what you gotta do, but I'm not working on that test again."

I could feel the eyes of my peers fixated on my head.

"We'll see."

After school, I went right home.

My mother asked me how the day went and I told her it went just fine. No reason to involve her in affairs concerning that monstrosity of a teacher. My father got home shortly before dinner, and, as usual, said nothing to me. I noted that we were having potatoes, corn, and roast beef again, and decided that at this meal I was just going to keep my mouth shut.

I glanced every now and then at my father, just out of sheer, morbid, curiosity. His face bristled with short whiskers and there was still some kind of faint streak of black across the top of one of his cheeks, probably some oil or something that he couldn't get off. He probably shaved every day before he left because at dinnertime every night he had the same stubble on his face. He was built thick; his arms were thick, his legs were thick, his torso was thick. Even his face was thick. Sometimes on weekends he would wear shirts that would reveal big muscles pretty much everywhere. I don't know how he got them or how he kept them. It had to something to do with his job, but I didn't really know what his job was, except that he was some kind of mechanic. He had a scar above his right eye that angled up towards his ear. I always wondered how far that scar went, and how he got it. I was terrified I might someday encounter the man that had bested my father. Of course, it was possible it was not in a fight that he got his scar. It seemed to me to be more likely that the dummy dropped a wrench on his head.

I didn't take my father to be a very bright man. He didn't do much. He wasn't about much. He woke up in the morning, put in his time, came home, ate dinner, watched TV, went to bed, and got up the next morning to do the same thing all over again. I just couldn't believe that someone could be content with this kind of existence. Is that really what life is about? Really? When I grew up, I was going to *do* something. I don't know what. *Anything* is better than this.

"I didn't see you in my classroom yesterday," Mr. Cavanaugh glared at me.

"Yea, I told you I wasn't com'n," I glared right back.

"I'll see you in my classroom after school today, then," Mr. Cavanaugh said. I saw his skinny little arm twitch and couldn't stop the corner of my lip turning into a smile. Mr. Cavanaugh misunderstood what it was that I thought was funny. "There is nothing funny about you not doing what you are told by an authority and there certainly is nothing funny about you throwing your life away because you're afraid others will find out about you. Are you a coward, Caleb?"

I couldn't fathom what on earth Mr. Cavanaugh meant by 'others finding out about me' but I did know that teachers shouldn't be calling their students 'cowards.'

"Yea, well at least I didn't get run out of the last place I worked, yellow-belly!" I blurted out, following with an uncomfortable laugh. I could hear gasps and other uncomfortable giggles amongst my peers and knew that I had landed a good one.

Mr. Cavanaugh said nothing, but looked at me intently, as if trying to guess what exactly I knew. After a long moment he said, "Caleb *Schnelling*--" he emphasized my last name--"You will be in my classroom at the end of the day today to correct your answers to my test or you will regret it."

"We'll see," I smirked.

At dinner that night I noticed that my father had another black smudge on his face. He made eye contact with me once as I was trying to size him up but he quickly lost interest and returned to his meal. My mother doted on him, giving him second helpings and pouring his drinks without him even asking. I thought it was disgusting, but I didn't dare speak my mind.

"Mis-ster Schnel-ling," Mr. Cavanaugh said, deliberating on each syllable.

"Yea?" I asked, cocking my head defiantly.

"Before you came to class today, I called your home and talked to your mother."

I glanced around at my friends. I couldn't believe this jackass would stoop this low *and* put it all out in front of the whole class. Totally unprofessional. I stared at him without replying, wishing to God that there was some kind of secret, heretofore unknown force that would carry death along my line of sight and bury it inside Mr. Cavanaugh's thin, elongated head. To my deep dismay, he did not drop dead, and instead continued.

"Your mother assures me that after school today, you will appear in my class to correct your test. I trust no further measures are necessary?" he asked. I was quite sure I saw the corner of his mouth twitch.

"Fat chance," I said.

At dinner, my mother asked me about it.

"This guy, he's got it out for me. He hates me."

"He's your teacher, and if he asks you to do some extra work after school every now and then, we expect that you'll do it. Schoolwork is your job, Caleb. Just like your dad gets up every day and works hard for this family, your job is to work hard at school so someday you can provide for your family, too."

I wasn't expecting this tact but it didn't really matter, I was still stewing in Mr. Cavanaugh's hatred for me.

"You know what he said to me in class the other day?" I asked. "He called me a *coward.*"

My father put his fork down and looked at me hard.

My mother glanced at him, but pressed on, "Even so, he's in charge, and he really thinks that you can correct the homework he said you would know about. It shouldn't take you very long, and you really haven't got a choice."

"He embarrassed me in front of all my friends," I moaned.

Without taking his eyes off me, my father stopped chewing.

"Well, that *is* unacceptable," my mother seemed to acquiesce.

"Maybe you should come to class and put him on the spot the way he put me on the spot," I suggested. I then explained a little more about how things went down.

After listening carefully to my spiel, my mother said, "I will be there after school tomorrow to make sure he doesn't do that kind of thing again. But you *will* be there to finish your work. He *is* your teacher, after all, and you should *not* be speaking back to him in class. Understood?" she said.

I nodded; I could still feel my father's eyes burning on me and did not dare speak back, even though I had no desire to allow Mr. Cavanaugh any kind of victory whatsoever. I would have preferred that she come and tell him off and I just came home, but this seemed the best I was going to get.

"What's his name again?" she asked me.

"Mr. Cavanaugh," I answered.

My father picked up his fork and continued eating, but his eyes were closed in slits, as if he was in deep thought. I

what was coming! I finished my work quickly and pretended to still be at work so that when the action went down, I could give it my undivided attention. It was really amazing how easy this stuff was. It was almost embarrassing how easy it was.

The door opened.

I turned my head and behold! It was my *father* who strode in.

I gulped.

My brain went into overdrive trying to figure out what was happening. Could it be that my father had pulled rank on my mother, and was here to take Mr. Cavanaugh's side? I could see it now: a confluence of hatred pouring over my head, overflowing beyond measure on my shoulders, down my arms, to my feet, drowning me. I broke out into a cold sweat.

"I heard you called my son a coward," my father snarled.

I looked at my father, genuinely perplexed. *What the hell*

> *"You're son is brilliant, and full of potential, but as it stands right now, he is a **coward**"*

half-prayed that God would make him stop; that kind of exertion would kill a guy like him, and while I didn't mind that prospect that much, I knew it would devastate my mother.

I told all my friends the next day what was going to go down but, as I ought to have expected, none of them seemed eager to stick around to watch. For his part, Mr. Cavanaugh had nothing to say to me during class, though I swear I detected a bit of smugness in how he carried himself. This probably had a lot to do with the silly thread-bared suit he wore every day. It was as if he was unaware of his own sense of self-importance. Did he think he was a professor, or something, and not a teacher of middle-school students? Anyway, that day it smacked of smugness more than normal, but I kept my mouth shut.

I showed up in his classroom after school and sat down in my desk. I didn't have anything to say to the man. He simply directed me to correct my answers from the test from earlier and returned to his desk. He had no idea

is going on, here?

Mr. Cavanaugh looked up from his work with a start, and his lanky body followed suit. In half a second he was standing at full height behind his desk. My father was already in front of the desk. The difference in scale suddenly struck me: my father had a good fifty to seventy-five pounds on Mr. Cavanaugh, despite the fact that Mr. Cavanaugh towered over him by a solid eight inches. Compared to my father, Cavanaugh was a twig of a man. Strike that. Compared to any other man, Cavanaugh was a twig.

I now became afraid that my father was going to kill Mr. Cavanaugh. I wondered what that would do to my reputation, and weighing the merits of each possibility, decided it best to pray that God would throw cold water on my father's hot temper. It was a difficult decision, since nothing would please me more than seeing Mr. Cavanaugh broken in half; if some other person could do the dirty deed so that I could be spared any of the blowback, I would have been delighted. On the other hand, if my father murdered my teacher, that would mean jail time for my father, and both would be out of my hair...

Mr. Cavanaugh surprised me.

"Yes, that's right. Your son is so afraid of what his friends will think of his intelligence that he won't do quality work. He's a coward," Mr. Cavanaugh said, jutting his chin out.

"Care to come around the desk and say that face to face?" my father asked.

"Sure," Mr. Cavanaugh replied. And lo and behold, he did.

"You're son is brilliant, and full of potential, but as it stands right now, he is a coward," Mr. Cavanaugh repeated.

The blow my father delivered to the chin of Mr. Cavanaugh was as startling to me as it assuredly was to Mr. Cavanaugh. I stood up abruptly, knocking my chair over behind me. But I was wrong; Mr. Cavanaugh was not startled. Yea, he fell back five feet from the shot, but he stepped forward immediately, without hesitation, and stood just two feet from my father. He turned his cheek so that my father had a clear shot at the one he hadn't hit, and said, with cheek, "How about *this* side, next?"

Now it was my father who was startled. He stepped back, looking at Mr. Cavanaugh in a new light. I knew that my father had hit Mr. Cavanaugh far harder than he had hit me, but Mr. Cavanaugh, Mr. Green-Bean Cavanaugh, seemed positively unfazed by the blow. It was almost as if he *liked* it. At this point, if I had to guess what my father was thinking, it was that he was face to face with a genuine lunatic. For my part, I still couldn't figure what it was that my father was doing there instead of my mother. It made no sense at all based on everything I knew about the man and our relationship.

"Riley Cavanaugh? From Pittsburgh?" my father said at last.

"The one and the same," Mr. Cavanaugh replied. Then, he added, "And unless I'm mistaken, you are *Jerry Schnelling*."

My father nodded; I swear I saw the corner of his lip rise.

My father spoke again, "What I heard is true, then?"

"Probably," Mr. Cavanaugh said. "There were several variants of the rumors. Your reputation, on the other hand, is dead-on accurate."

A trickle of blood descended down Mr. Cavanaugh's chin,

but he hadn't yet shown any hint that he had felt even the tiniest bit of pain. I was doing all I could to try to understand this remarkable chain of events. My father's fists relaxed.

"You say my son is brilliant, and full of potential?" my father asked him.

"That's right," Mr. Cavanaugh replied.

"And you would know," my father said, to my deep confusion.

"I suppose I would," Mr. Cavanaugh said.

"But also a coward," my father added.

"You know *why* I said that," Mr. Cavanaugh said.

My father smiled a knowing smile and uttered a mystery, "Very well then, you have my permission to do what is necessary."

"I thank you for your trust," Mr. Cavanaugh answered.

I felt like I had to interject, "Aren't you going to finish him off or something? School is going to be unbearable now!"

My father turned his gaze upon me, and with a glint in his eye, told me, "You see this scar?" At this, he drew his finger along the edges of it on his forehead. "This is the man that gave it to me, a long, long time ago. Ol' Riley here is what we call a 'ringer.' If he had wanted to, he could put me down like a rabid dog, right here and now, and he wouldn't break a sweat. That about right, *Mr. Cavanaugh*?"

Mr. Cavanaugh was initially silent, but then seemed obliged to add something, winking, "That was years ago. I'm older now, and not as fit as you. Today, I would break a sweat."

"And the rumors?" my father said.

"*Probably* true," Mr. Cavanaugh dead-panned.

My father looked back and forth between me and Mr. Cavanaugh for a few moments and then, bizarrely, addressed me thusly: "You listen to Mr. Cavanaugh and do what he says. If he says you're brilliant, you most likely are. Don't worry about your friends. In a decade, they will amount to nothing. You listen to him, and you'll be somebody. You understand?"

Knowing nothing else to do, I nodded.

My father extended his hand to Mr. Cavanaugh, who took it, and holding it firmly, and said, "You did fine work with the Findlay Affair, Mr. Schnelling. Probably even saved some lives. I hope you know that there were many that noticed--and remain grateful."

My father shrugged, "Just did what was right."

"All we can try to do," Mr. Cavanaugh said.

My father nodded in agreement, and stepped back, and excused himself from the room, but not before first telling me to finish my homework. I looked back and forth between my father and Mr. Cavanaugh as he left, wondering if I had ever known either of them.

I was alone with Mr. Cavanaugh.

"Your father is a great man," Mr. Cavanaugh said to me.

I stood there, silent.

"I gave him that scar, but it was an accident. He was only protecting your mother," he explained. "There was a protest--well, never mind. It's very complicated. It was a misunderstanding between him and me, and there was a big crowd. We were both on the same side, but working it from different angles. It was a long time ago."

I didn't know what to say. It was all very perplexing.

"He's brilliant, you know. An engineer of the finest quality, and a man of strict principle, even willing to put his body on the line if it comes to it. That hasn't always been the best career move, but there are hundreds, if not thousands of people, who would want your father in their corner if it came down to *any* kind of fight. I'm one of them."

"I didn't know," I said softly.

"*I* did, or at least suspected before he walked through that door, confirming it. The apple doesn't fall far from the tree, as they say. Go home and ask him about the Findlay Affair, *Mr.* Caleb Schnelling. That's my last assignment of the day," he instructed me.

That night at supper I looked down at my plate and kept my eyes there. I didn't even bother sending furtive glances in the direction of my father. The man was an utter mystery to me. His regard for me was unfathomable and strange. Out of the corner of my eye, I could see my father and mother holding hands, while each ate with their free hand.

Finally, I completed my assignment: "Dad? Can you tell me about the Findlay Affair?"

And for five hours straight, he did just that.

———————————————

A MODEST CONSIDERATION

by Chaka Heinze

If there is no God, if we are accidents of time created not with purpose, but rather evolved as a byproduct of the collision of certain forces of nature (the universe's refuse if you will) then there is no point to humankind. We are merely consumers of other accidental byproducts of nature (which happen, by chance, to provide the exact nutrients the human body needs) and the whole majestic, magnificently balanced universe exists for no reason other reason except to advance forward in time until the whole thing is destroyed by the next great accidental collision. If humankind exists without purpose and our existence is limited to our brief inhabitation of this fleshy vessel, then I submit to you that a person's greatest ambition must be to achieve maximum happiness (which we shall refer to as "self-gratification" for the purpose of this discourse) and our every effort should be to attain that goal. In short, every individual should grab all they can and as much as they can, while they can.

Let us toss aside conscience (or at least ignore it mightily) and every other obstacle that might hinder us in the pursuit of this chief aim! Anything and anyone that does not add to our happiness is folly and a waste of our finite time in this current fortuitous epoch of clashing matter that erupted into existence by some unknown hocus pocus. I apologize, "hocus pocus" connotes the existence of some invisible (or other realmed) magician, suffice it to say that at some point in the past history of the visible universe there was nothing and then matter suddenly, inexplicably appeared. Now, back to the matter at hand.

Babies have already achieved the highest end of accidental man, they exist in a perpetual state of desiring instant and complete self-gratification, no matter the detriment to others around them. As a matter of fact, it seems that we must become better at imitating them in order to achieve maximum self-gratification for ourselves. But since they are already the pinnacle of man (in a world where honor, achievement, purpose and charity only exist where they might benefit the individual's gratification) we shall leave them and move on to that stage in development in which we transition from babe to self-aware individual. It is from this perilous peak of awareness that we must stand on the mount of decision and recognize that it would be the height of folly to pursue anything but self-gratification when our time on this doomed orb is so limited.

For those who are able, they should lie, cheat and steal with impunity and avoid detection at all costs for this is the quickest way to obtain the desired effect of instant gratification. Please don't live as if someone is keeping track of your deeds; it's important to force such archaic limitations from your thoughts. The acquisition of your chief desires may indeed inhibit another's desire, but their needs are of no consequence unless they aid in furthering your own gratification. If you are able to infringe on another's self-gratification while increasing your own, then by all means, do so! Perhaps carry a picture of an infant around to remind you of the goal of your endeavors. But for those of you unable to master the evolutionary stricture called conscience or who simply lack the innate capacity to employ these abilities in a way that benefits ourselves, you should look to your employments, relationships, hobbies and inborn desires to achieve your aim.

Unfortunately, it is still too often the case that one must work in order to eat. And since eating leads to gratification, it is vital that one discovers a way to acquire food, shelter and the other necessities of existence. For those to whom lying, cheating and stealing is repugnant, they must either find a way to be supported by another person or by a government agency, or they must find gainful employment—preferably employment that achieves maximum gratification. It is important to remember that, as an accident of the collision of forces, no allegiance is owed, so please choose an employment unencumbered by any limiting moral responsibility. The most you can hope for in your limited time frame is gratification, therefore it is not necessary that the employment benefit anyone or anything else as long as it is paying a living wage. One does not need to "save the world" (or the children for that matter) unless doing so will deposit more gratification currency in the universal bank of me, myself and I. Consider the picture of the infant; life is all about you.

Without an almighty presence violating the prime directive of self-gratification at any cost, we must reconsider the way we approach our relationships. If you are able to maintain a relationship with anyone or anything that is immensely gratifying to you even if it causes the other party distress, then you are well on your way to devolving into that infantile creature from whence you sprang. There is no divine purpose behind a relationship; they

exist solely to further your ambitions. It is necessary to continually weigh any relationship on the balance of pleasure or pain. If a relationship causes any amount of pain or consternation, flee from it. If a relationship is pleasurable, remain in it—but keep an eye out, the moment that pleasure runs out it is necessary for you to run out along with it. Relationships are made simple when one has a clear worldview unhindered by any constraint but the god of self.

And it goes without saying that your hobbies are your own and an area in which you can continually focus on your need for gratification. The only law (and I apologize for using a word that may or may not be laden with judgment for some) for the desirable life of an evolved being is the consideration of whether or not the hobby brings pleasure. A hobby is immensely desirable since it can be undertaken without the need for dreadful interactions which can limit personal enjoyment and therefore, in the privacy of shelter, one is free to enjoy whichever hobby ones whims, desires or caprices dictate. But I'm preaching to the choir aren't I? Your hobbies and darker pleasures are an area in which you excel the best at heeding the infantile whimsy of self-gratification. Well done, there is no need to speak on it further.

As my pleasure is waning in continuing with this discourse, it is time to leave off with a few final comments. If carried out to its logical conclusion, the idea of humankind existing as a result of a biological accident which occurred many millennium ago pleasantly strips our lives of both context and meaning. While many will undoubtedly proclaim that the idea of self-gratification being the chief objective of our existence is a juvenile intention reserved for infants, I take offense; keep your contrived moral judgments to yourself. I say live and let live (so long as your living extracts not one ounce of pleasure from my own). My friends, the possibilities for pleasure are infinite, while your lifespan is but a breath. I am certain that when you thoroughly and logically examine the "purpose" of accidental man, you will draw no other conclusion than the one I have set forth: If there is no God, no purpose, no greater import for our actions or inactions then we may as well "eat and drink, for tomorrow we die."

Think about it.

THERE ARE OTHER THINGS TO DO IN SWITZERLAND

by Jim Yarbrough

Looking back on it, it was odd. This friendship. Jason and me. He proudly unfettered, rationalistic, and dispassionate. Me a Christian, a people-person, a broad historical sweeper. Me married with two kids. He a childless widower. Two engineers working in the same firm for over 20 years.

He lounged in his favorite brown-purple corduroy overstuffed easy chair which appeared to have come over to the New World on one of the first ships to Plymouth. His pricey apartment nestled in one of the city's posh, heavily treed districts. He always said he couldn't afford it. But he did.

"You know I invited you over for a reason."

"Does your objectivism ever allow you to invite me for no reason?" I chuckled, sitting on the less comfortable divan.

"You know what I mean, Roy." He flashed his wry smile. But then it evaporated. "I'm dying."

I couldn't say I was totally surprised. Since he retired a few months ago, we'd been having coffee weekly at that little bistro near his neighborhood; he had been looking drawn, grayer.

"What is it?"

"MS."

I tried to be careful, but I could sense myself becoming frustrated. I thought I knew what was coming next. "Jason, MS is terrible yes, but now it can be a controllable disease."

"I'm already losing energy. I'm becoming degraded, less sharp on my feet. My doctor says even with aggressive treatments – injections with interferon betas and glatiramer acetate, new pills, steroids...I don't know -- it would be a constant battle to maintain myself for another 10 or 15 years."

"So?"

"You mean 'so,' as in what else is new and why can't I cope? Or 'so' as in what am I going to do about it?"

"I know you want to talk about the latter question, so: what do you think you want to do?"

He rose and walked to his desk, with its polished dark walnut top abutting the bay window looking out onto the hickory and maple woods in the broad creek bed. An occasional jogger on the partially occluded path opposite the creek was the only break in the sylvan peace. He fumbled in the top right drawer and extracted a large manila file folder. He handed it to me as he returned to his chair. I opened it.

"There's this place near Zurich. Switzerland." As I leafed through the slick company brochure conveniently printed in

German, French, Italian, and English, I saw peripherally he was anxious for my impressions. "It's very tasteful, luxurious. As you see. Run very professionally. Completely regulated by the Government. There are counselors. Even pastoral staff, Roy. They don't rush you. You take all the time you need. Then when you're ready, you go into a very homey-type room, and you give yourself the injection."

I unhurriedly finished my scan of the brochure. "It's my engineering side, Jason. Let's go back to first principles."

He frowned.

"Objectivism: the belief that reason is the absolute in a person's life. His own happiness is the moral purpose of his life. Productive achievement in the external world is his noblest activity. See similarities with utilitarianism. We've been through this – how many times over the years? But have I got that about right?"

"Don't you see the flaw in your thinking, Roy? Why are you so afraid of death? I'm not. It's just a ceasing of functioning. A...an inevitable wearing down of the machinery. Why not phase it out before it completely fails? You're a Christian. You're not supposed to be afraid of death."

"For the umpteenth time, I'm not afraid of death for me, Jason. But I am afraid of it for you. You and I are not machines."

"That's your worldview, not mine."

This is where we had ended up time and time again. Only this time our conversation had more of an edge to it. Because he was trying to cope with his mortality. And I was trying to help him cope with coping.

"I want you to go with me to Zurich."

I didn't hesitate. "You know what? I would love to go to Zurich with you. And every minute of our time together I'd be trying to talk you out of it. I would not stop. It would be really pleasant for you."

"That's a totally bullying point of view, Roy." He was sulking, little boy-like.

"All this segues really well back to the first question: So, why can't you try to cope? And you know why that question is so important to me? Do you know?" I found my voice rising, my throat clinching, and my eyes watering. "Because you are my friend. My long-time, close friend. And I love you."

"So this is all about selfish emotion? Chemical reactions producing emotion..." Jason hung his head, encapsulated.

"Chemically induced? We humans are physically wonderfully made, yes. But the human side of emotion is more than mechanics. And we humans – including me -- undoubtedly are selfish. But emotions are about much more than human selfishness. The Bible says we are made in God's image, and throughout Scripture we see God – the Father or the Son -- expressing emotion. He was sad he made Saul King of Israel. Jesus was excited at the faith of the Centurion, and he truly was pleased the rich young man followed the commandments. "

Jason peered over the desk, out the window.

"There's another thing. It's about life – and emotion. At the end of Genesis 1 after He had made the heavens and earth and all the teeming life, He was...pleased. Scripture says 'God saw all He had made, and it was very good.' Emphasis on the very. Did you ever think how precious any life is if it makes the omnipotent Creator happy? You and I are part of that life, Jason."

"I know. I know you believe in God. I know you see a connection in all this."

"Our deaths are not what God wanted. In our free will, we fell. Now we die. But what He wants for us is what we should want for ourselves – to be alive and love Him."

Enough I thought. I hadn't been this scripturally direct with him...ever. "Jason, I don't know what's in store for me or you even tomorrow, but I know this: for as long as I am alive and wherever you and I are, I'll be your friend. I'll invest in you. So, please... please don't end that friendship."

He looked up from the floor with one of his patented, ironic grins.

I don't know yet if that marked a turning point in our relationship or – more importantly – a turning point in his relationship with God. But I do know there was something...something... more vulnerable and open about Jason after that. He was a rounded corner rather than a razor-sharp angular barb.

Why had it been so hard for me to say to him straight-out in the previous 20 years that he was my friend and I would always love him?

THE GODLESS ONE

Robert W Cely

I am the Godless one!
Hear my empty creeds
I bow to none or nothing
Behold my sordid deeds
Right and wrong like potter's clay
I mold for my own ends
What's good today is cursed the next
And only fools contend

I am the Godless one!
I preach the great void
There is none to cling to
All is devoid
Space is cold, earth inflamed
No angels trim the skies
I searched for God, I found him not
He is the great, "I Lie"

I am the Godless one!
Fear ye all who live
Don't barter for forgiveness
I have none to give
Two of your eyes for one of mine
I am the hand of wrath
More blood for blood more death for life
Will be my epitaph

I am the Godless one!
I am the self-made man
There is none I owe allegiance to
Beneath no flag to stand
This castle built by my own hands
With vast and empty halls
A vacant court, I lone preside
The echoes serve my call

I am the Godless one!
I ravage all in sight
There is no food to fill me
My endless appetite
One banquet set, one table long
The flesh and blood devoured
The crimson drink, the carnal feast
All praise the witching hour

I am the Godless one!
The king of all the beasts
A debtor to the father ape
That first climbed from the trees
I eat my fill, I mate and die
One link of endless chain
Survival looms impulse supreme
Luck, our queen who reigns

I am the Godless one!
I only see despair
I only grasp at misery
I only clutch the air
There is no love, there is no hope
There is only death and fear
There is no need for Hell to consume
I have found it here

WHEN GOD DREW NEAR

fiction by **Chaka Heinze**

Sometimes God is a distant phantom, amorphous in form, indistinct from the realm of those things both seen and unseen which hover in a remote place well beyond understanding. Sometimes He is a definition, a commandment, a distant history that is truth but which seems separate and apart from our present reality. Always, our best understanding is a dim reflection of the great truth of the Creator of all things. But sometimes... sometimes when he pulls back the veil we see: Father, friend, lover, broken heart, comforter, rescuer, avenger, champion, artist, master craftsman, great musician, poet,

dreamer and...healer. Sometimes God draws so near that if he were solid form, we could reach out and touch him.

And once upon a time, God drew near.

The night had ended routinely enough. A family game was played and the youngest of the children mastered both bowling and basketball on the Wii. His mom tickled him at bedtime and together they laughed before a prayer and a goodnight kiss. And that night, as she closed her eyes thankful to be able to tuck her children safely in their beds, she was clueless that God was about to step directly into this ordinary scene.

Between the witching and the waking hour on an ordinary night the little boy's heart began to beat chaotically and the Great Healer watched from his lofty place.

"Shall I go to him, master?" a glimmering presence hovering beside him asked in a voice tinged with music.

The Great Healer shook his massive head as he answered. "Not yet, child."

The boy's implanted device sensed the chaos of his heart and set out to correct it with a current of electricity. But the device was limited; though programmed to deliver a shock to an ailing heart it had not the intelligence to fix a vital connection from itself to the heart and the current failed to reach its intended destination. The electric shock improperly discharged in the boy, jolting his body into spasms, and his heartbeat further deteriorated.

The glimmering presence tore his eyes away from the boy dying in his bed on an ordinary night and looked to his master. The tears in his master's eyes reflected the scene below. "Shall I make final preparations on his room, master?"

The Great Healer's gaze never left the boy. "Not yet, child," he answered.

Each time the device sensed the failure of the boy's heart it increased the voltage of the charge to shock the heart into a normal rhythm. Six times it jolted the boy's body. Six times it failed. After the last time, the device continued to gather information, but no further shocks were delivered.

As the boy grew still, silent tears streamed down the face of the glimmering presence. The transition of a mortal to the realm immortal was never an ordinary event in the eyes of the Master or his servants. "And so it's finished," the servant stated simply.

The Master Healer's face quivered with emotion and then a smile touched his mouth and soon it stretched across his face and the light of his face glowed. The fierce brightness pierced the membrane separating the realm of seen and unseen, heaven and earth, God and Man. "Not yet, child," the Master Healer responded as he stepped into the cluttered bedroom of the little boy.

The servant watched in awe as the Master Healer stood at the edge of the boy's bed and reached out to lay his hand on the boy's heart. Lowering himself to the boy's ear he whispered, "Not yet, child." And the boy began to breathe again. And then he began to convulse. And then he began to scream. And his screams woke his mother sleeping in the other room. As she reached her son, the Master Healer stepped out of time and back to his timeless realm where the servant continued

to study him with awe.

And the extraordinary traversing the ordinary shone the light of truth on dim understanding. The idea itself emitting a luminescence all its own. The distance between creator and created breached by a mere thought in the mind of the omnipotent Master Healer. "The child's story is not all told," the servant commented delightedly.

The Master Healer pulled him close in his familiar embrace. "Not yet, child," he answered.

Physical or phantom? Distance ebbing and flowing according to the impact of emotional eddies disturbing our peace from within and without, but, in truth, He is not made and unmade according to our fancies and whims. He is faithful. And sometimes—sometimes he rends the heavens to remind us that this is so.

_____

THE CHALLENGES OF
NARRATIVE
APOLOGETICS

by Jamie Greening

As I understand it, narrative (or literary) apologetics is the task of defending or propagating the Christian worldview through story. Narrative apologetics is at the opposite end of the apologetics spectrum from propositional, or debatable apologetics. The two are not in competition, nor are they adversaries. Indeed, they are colleagues. No, not colleagues. They are sisters. However, narrative apologetics faces at least two unique challenges which are different from those faced by its bullet pointed and diagram drawing sister.

One challenge is unique to Christian narrative while the other is universal to all writing. Of course, challenge is simply a nice way of saying that something is difficult, but not impossible. These challenges are not Everests, which only a select few can even dare to scale and overcome. These challenges are more like the tree in the backyard. Most people can climb it, but not everyone will think it worth the effort.

Let us take the universal challenge first. I say universal because it is a challenge that applies to almost every story ever told. This is the challenge to move beyond cliché. There are no new ideas, really, and everything has already been written in some form or other, and this has given rise to cliché. By cliché I do not only mean tired tropes like describing the young protagonist as, "a diamond in the rough." I also mean the plot or character cliché—the lone ranger, the mysterious stranger, the desperate housewife, the vixen, the well-meaning pastor and a thousand other clichés.

Every genre has its own cliché. Once upon a time, starting your story with, "It was a dark and stormy night," or "Once upon a time," for that matter had never really been done before. But now, it is just a cliché. Bodices ripping, zombies attacking, lawyers covering-up, politicians lying, and spaceships crashing are all clichés. Yet, they are vital to their respective genres. I dare anyone to write a compelling space drama without some problem or nuanced description of the blasted spaceship. To me it seems like the spaceship always has problems. It simply must happen. The trick for the writer is to use the cliché in a way that it doesn't sound like one.

You should never write, "It was a dark and stormy night." However, you'd better get the weather into your story somehow. In the first draft of my new novel I'm working through I spent almost an entire week with the language about rain in Western Washington, which is almost a cliché all by itself, and the car stuck in the mud it created. It turned out to be one of my favorite parts of the story. It was also hard to write because so much of it was wrought with cliché.

The trick is to embrace the cliché without sounding like a cliché.

A great example of this is J. K. Rowling. Whatever else you might think of her, she turned the cliché of teenage angst in a boarding school into something so beloved that it now has its own theme park. At their heart, The Harry Potter novels are nothing but one cliché after another, rife with a Merlin, the orphaned child, mysterious powers, time travel, the chosen one, and Armageddon. The Harry, Ron, Hermione triangle could be retitled , Luke, Han, and Leia: The Early Years. Rowling, though, is a great writer because she writes in such a way that makes you forget the cliché.

In the Christian narrative world our great problem is we don't dress up our cliché very well. Our heroes are often too perfect with no crisis of faith or doubt of any kind. Add to this the cliché of knowing exactly what is evil and what is not. Christian writers have the hardest time letting the reader decide who or what is wrong. I struggled with this in my most recent novel because, quite frankly, we have convictions that tell us how the world ought to be. But there it is, sitting there on the page, and it reads like a cliché.

The worst cliché we abuse is the quick end to a spiritual renewal. I did that one time in a short story with a character I really cared about. I didn't spend the time working on her spiritual struggle long enough. The result was she came around to a place of faith, literarily speaking, far too fast. I corrected some of this when she appeared again in another story, but the damage had already been done.

Church is a great big cliché in our Christian narratives as well. Church is almost always good, sweet, and wholesome in our novels. The problem is, that is not how church really is, and readers know that. Most Christians have a real hard time, at some point or other, with their own church. Our sense of duty and calling, though, hinders us from treating it that way. We don't want to be guilty of painting Christ's beloved in a negative light so we paint her always as the pristine bride. Or, we paint her as Gomer, the harlot Hosea was shackled to. The truth, and the solution to the cliché, is somewhere in the middle.

There are many other Christian clichés, but this is just a sampling of them. Our job is not to run away from these, instead run with them. While you run around with these, give them room to break free for a moment and do unexpected things. Again, I'll use Rowling because almost everyone knows the story. From the very beginning we all knew that Albus Dumbledore would die. The mentor always has to die so the student can grow up. It is a story fact. What did Rowling do to make it interesting? Well, (spoiler) she had him killed by someone he trusted, who did it at his order, who was a good guy all along but had to play like he was a bad one.

That is good writing, and an amazing take on the Judas cliché.

If she can do it with wizards, we ought to be able to do it even better with the Gospel.

May I humbly suggest that such writing requires hard work and determination? It also requires a commitment to storytelling that transcends a desire for apologetics. If you try to defend everything in your story, you will end up defending nothing—or at least nothing anyone would want to read. Leave the explicit telling of everything in the hands of those who are doing the propositional apologetics. As a storyteller, your job is different. If you can't stand that nuance, then you need to be doing something else, like making Powerpoint slides with bullets.

A Christian narrative apologists should have writing great literature as a goal, not just telling Christian stories.

So cliché is one challenge. The other challenge for narrative apologetics, the one that is unique to the Christian worldview, is the question of who will read our stories. In other words, the literary apologist must work not only at getting readers but getting the right kind of readers.

Here is what I'm getting at. Every writer has a particular target audience he or she believes will have a predisposition for buying the stories. Amish love stories are targeted at thirty-five to fifty-five year old women and literary agents. I'm not kidding, literary agents love Amish love stories. You know why? They sell! They sell a lot, because most of the books in this country are bought and read by that particular demographic.

Church health books are marketed toward evangelical pastors.

Comic books are targeted at twenty something year old men who still live with their parents and don't have meaningful work.

Every writer has a target audience. However, that being said, every writer will willingly sell to anyone who buys it, no questions asked. The goal of writing is to have readers.

While this is true for the Christian narrative apologists, we have a different ultimate goal. Our desire is to have a particular kind of reader; the kind of reader that goes beyond target audiences and demographic concerns. As apologists, we want someone who doesn't share our worldview to read our story. We want that person to read it and

enter into a dialogue with it. It is not enough for us to sell a book and get an audience. If we don't get a certain kind of audience, then we have failed.

This is different from every other writing genre. When Beverly Lewis writes nostalgically about the Amish, she doesn't want you to become Amish. That is not her goal. She wants to entertain you. I'll grant that she wants to entertain you in a Christian worldview, but she still primarily wants to entertain. Stephen King doesn't want to convince you that psychopathic ghosts are real. He just has a passion for telling a certain kind of story. He wants to entertain you. Marvel Comics has no desire for you to become an agent of S.H.I.E.L.D.

In contrast, the Christian narrative apologist wants the reader to be changed by the experience, or at least challenged. The Christian literary apologist cannot be content with a target audience of people who agree with his or her worldview and good sales. If the conversation that comes out of the material doesn't lean skeptics or doubt-ers closer in toward the truth of the Gospel, then the endeavor is definitively unsuccessful.

Here comes the tricky challenging part. How do you find that audience?

That question is not as easy as you might think. First, to write the kind of material that an unbeliever might read generally requires an edginess that traditional Christian publishers would not publish, and more to the point, Christian bookstores will not carry. Ask yourself if something as wonderful and great as The Chronicles of Narnia or A Wrinkle in Time, both written with a definite Christian perspective and a powerful apologetic message, would ever be accepted for publication today by Christian publishers. I think the answer is no.

Too many witches.

Too much paganism.

The symbolism is not overtly explained.

Space travel and other worlds don't fit in with the chronology of Genesis and so many other problems.

I just don't think today's Christian publishers would ever touch it today.

So publication through Christian outlets is nearly impossible for reaching a mass audience of the unconvinced. This is an indictment against Christian media and those of us (me included) who consume it. From an artistic perspective, we are like spoiled children who insist upon only having only cheap grape jelly with peanut butter on our sandwich, with the crust cut off, for lunch. It is not media's fault. They give us what we want, and they know what we want because we keep buying the same tame stuff over and over again.

On the flipside, because we desire our material to carry spiritual connotations, it will be missing many of the ingredients that mainstream publishing companies will want. Explicit sexual activity, profanity, and fatalism are not the kinds of things we want, or are willing, to write about. That ties the hands of the narrative apologists, because those are the very things that drive sales of most books. If we give them what they want, they will not get what they need.

There is a reason why almost everyone in the world (except me) read Fifty Shades of Grey, and it wasn't for the plot.

This leaves the narrative apologist in a publishing pickle. She goes too far in her prose to be published by her brothers and sisters, but she doesn't go far enough for those who market for the key target audience. Therefore, something else must be done.

I have come to believe that the solution to this chasm are the bridges we can build with alternate material. The single greatest thing that a narrative apologist can do is to intentionally write stories and novels that carry little or no spiritual or biblical message. These stories should be well written, polished, and excellent. By writing these types of stories, a writer can generate goodwill at worst, and possibly fans at best, who will then desire to read more from that writer. That is most of our experiences as readers. We pick up a book by an author, we read the book, we like it, and then we go find more books by that writer.

That is the best way to solve the audience problem.

The catch is that this strategy takes time, because stories do not just crank themselves out overnight. Ask me in ten years or so if it has worked for me. It might take that long to find out.

Jamie Greening served as a pastor in Washington State for 14 years. Now he resides in the Texas Hill Country with his wife and daughters and devotes his time to writing and baking biscuits. He is the author of *The Little Girl Waits, The Haunting of Pastor Butch Gregory and Other Short Stories*, various short stories including *Speculation, Jolly Rogers, The Land Begins to Heal*, and *The Last Message*. He also authors the Deep Cove monster series including *Deep Cove, Deep Cove: The Party Crasher, The Deep Cove Lineage*, and *The Deep Cove Investigation*. He blogs as Pastor Greenbean at jamiegreening.com and continues to speak, preach, and teach wherever he may have opportunity.

The One Who Always Was

Derek Elkins

A whispered air, a sheltered room,
the name inside a wind-swept bloom

The transformed heart, the artist pure,
where dream, desire and death converge

A fragrant breath, a tethered womb,
the dearth of death's enlightened tomb

The promised wealth, the hidden cure,
where power, calm and frailty merge

And in the heart where shadows dwell,
where darkness claims its throne for hell

A leader's pause reigns down the hall and
causes mansion's rise to fall
So comes the one who always was

Name Me

Callie Smith

Running toward an empty place,
Seeking tracks I cannot trace,
Staring at an unknown face,
Name me.

Hiding though I'm in a crowd,
Speechless though I call aloud,
Choking waves are crashing wild,
Find me.

If I'm running will you chase me,
If I'm hiding will you seek me?
Without you, I'm nameless, soulless,
Without you, I'm aimless, goalless.

Without you I'm wasting time,
Running a race, no finish line,
You are my home, my hope, my sign,
Save me.